The Boxcar Childre

THE GREAT BICYCLE RACE MYSTERY

created by
GERTRUDE CHANDLER WARNER

Illustrated by Charles Tang

Albert Whitman & Company
Chicago, Illinois

Contents

THE GREAT BICYCLE
RACE MYSTERY

CHAPTER 1

And Grandfather, Too

"H . . . e . . . l . . p . . ."
Benny Alden spelled out the letters of the first word on the sign in the front window. He looked up at his oldest sister, Jessie. "Help! That's what it says, doesn't it?" he cried. "Is someone in trouble?"

Twelve-year-old Jessie laughed. "Don't worry, Benny," she told her youngest brother. "No one's in trouble. From what the sign says, it's a mountain that needs help."

"A mountain?" asked Benny, who was six. "How can you help a mountain?"

The four Aldens — Benny, Jessie, Violet, and Henry — had just stopped their bicycles in front of Greenfield Wheels. It was a bicycle shop in their hometown of Greenfield. But they hadn't ridden their bikes to the shop. They'd walked, because Henry's bicycle had gotten a flat tire as they were riding into town.

Violet, who was ten, came to Benny's rescue. "The sign says, 'Help Save Eagle Mountain. Join the Race to Save the Park. Ask Inside and Thelma Will Tell You How to Sign Up.' "

"Let's ask, then," said Benny.

"We can do that while I get a new tube to fix my flat tire," agreed fourteen-year-old Henry.

Violet held the door open for Henry and his bike, and they all went into the shop.

Inside, bicycles of every kind and color lined both walls: rows of bikes on the floor and rows of bikes hanging from the ceiling on hooks. There were racks displaying wheels and seats and water bottles and helmets and all kinds of bike equipment.

Benny stared. He'd been in the bike shop before, but he always forgot how many bikes it had. As they walked down the narrow aisle at the center of the store, Jessie ran her hand over the cool silver of a handlebar. Violet stopped to admire a purple bicycle. Purple was Violet's favorite color.

Just as they reached the counter at the back, a voice said, "I'm Louis. What can I do for you?"

Henry looked around. He couldn't see who had spoken. "I have a flat tire," he said.

"Ah." A short, wiry man popped out from around an open door at the back of the narrow space behind the counter. A sign taped to the wall by the door read REPAIR AREA. EMPLOYEES ONLY. The man wiped his grease-stained hands on a rag that hung on a hook below the sign.

He peered over the counter at Henry's flat tire. "Hmmm," he said. "Interesting old bike you've got there."

"Thank you," said Henry. "I want to fix the flat tire."

The man nodded. He said, "Okay. Bring

it on back. But I have to tell you, I'm not sure a patch will work. That tire is almost worn out. You need a new tire."

"I thought I might," said Henry.

Opening the half door at one end of the counter, the man motioned for Henry to push his bike through.

"We need to know about helping the mountain, too," Benny spoke up.

"Helping the mountain?" said the man, looking puzzled.

"Like the sign in the window says," explained Benny.

"Oh!" said the man. "You want to know about the bike ride. Thelma!" He shouted out the name so suddenly that all the Aldens jumped a little.

A voice shouted back, "Don't shout! I'm busy. I'm in the middle of a broken spoke."

"That's Thelma," the man said. "Replacing a broken spoke. If she can't fix your bike, it can't be fixed."

"That's right!" she said, popping into the doorway. She paused to wipe her hands. Unlike Louis, she wasn't covered in smudges of grease. She was a little taller than Louis, with sandy hair pulled back in a French braid. Tiny silver earrings shaped like bicycles dangled from her ears.

"What's up?" she asked, stepping aside so Louis could wheel Henry's bike into the repair area.

"We want to know about the mountain," Benny said.

"Eagle Mountain?" asked Thelma.

"Yes, and the bike race," Violet said.

Thelma smiled. She said, "It's not really a race. The race is against time. We're running out of time to raise money to save Eagle Mountain. This is a bike ride to raise money to help buy it."

"What's going to happen to the mountain?" asked Violet.

"A *developer* is trying to buy it," said Thelma, wrinkling her nose as if the word had a bad smell. "Her name is May Whatney and she wants to buy Eagle Mountain, cut down most of the trees, and put in lots of roads and a golf course and a bunch of big houses. The present owner has always let the public hike through his property, but now he needs money and wants to sell Eagle Mountain to the highest bidder. If we can raise enough money, we might be able to convince the state to buy it and turn it into a wilderness park."

"How will the bike ride help?" Henry asked.

"It's a three-day ride. It starts at Eagle Mountain and it ends up at the state capitol. We'll hold a rally on the steps of the capitol building and give the money we've raised to the governor," Thelma said.

"But how does that make money?" Jessie questioned.

"Every rider will have to pay an entry fee and raise at least a dollar a mile for the trip," Thelma went on. "The riders will ride a certain number of miles each day and camp each night at a camp set up by the volunteers. Tents and food have been donated by different organizations, but all the riders have to provide their own sleeping bag, clothes, and bike."

"Don't forget the raffle!" Louis called from the back.

"Right," said Thelma. "For every five dollars over the minimum amount you raise, you get a raffle ticket with your name on it. At the end of the ride, there will be a drawing and one of the riders will win a custom-made Sergio Spokes titanium racing bike. The only rule is that you have to ride the whole way to be eligible for the raffle."

"Wow," said Henry. "It sounds great."

Violet nodded, and Benny said, "I want to save the mountain."

"Where do we sign up?" asked Jessie.

Thelma pulled a stack of papers from a drawer. "Here are the forms. Just fill them out and mail them in with the entry fee. You can hand in the money you raise on the day of the race or you can mail it in, too."

"Great," said Henry.

"Bike's fixed," said Louis, reappearing in the doorway with Henry's bike.

"That was fast," said Jessie.

"Practice," said Louis. He smiled, revealing a chipped front tooth. "I'll show you how to do it if you sign up for the race. Every bike rider should know how to fix a flat tire."

Benny gave a little skip of excitement. "This will be fun," he declared. "We'll ride for miles and miles and miles and camp out in tents and raise lots of money for the mountain *and* we'll fix flat tires. I can hardly wait."

The other Aldens laughed. So did Thelma and Louis. "That's the spirit," Thelma said. "I can tell that this is going to be a great bike race."

"Sounds like a terrific idea," said Grandfather later that night at dinner. "Eagle Mountain is a wonderful place. We used to go hiking there when I was a boy."

"I want to ride in the race, too," said Soo Lee. "My dad says I'm an expert rider!" Soo Lee was a cousin of the Aldens. She lived in Greenfield with their uncle Joe and aunt Alice, who'd adopted her.

The Aldens had been orphans, too.

They'd lived in an old abandoned boxcar in the woods. That was where they had found their dog, Watch. And that was where their grandfather, who had been searching for his grandchildren, had found them. He'd taken them to live with him in his big old house in Greenfield and put the boxcar behind the house so they could visit it whenever they wanted.

Now Soo Lee was spending the night at her cousins' house, as she often did. Soo Lee and Violet were good friends, and she was sitting next to Violet at the dinner table. Mrs. McGregor, their housekeeper, had just finished serving them fried chicken, mashed potatoes, and corn on the cob.

But Jessie was frowning. "I don't know," she said. "I don't know if any of us can go on the bike ride, come to think of it."

"What? Why not?" cried Violet.

"Because it says on the forms that you have to be eighteen to ride, or you have to have an adult ride with you," Jessie said.

For a moment, everyone was silent.

Then Benny cried, "It's not fair!"

Henry glanced at Soo Lee. "Maybe we could ask Aunt Alice or Uncle Joe to come with us," he said.

"Maybe," said Soo Lee. But she didn't sound as if she thought they would be able to do it.

But then Grandfather Alden smiled and said, "I'll go on the bike ride with you."

Benny was so surprised that he dropped the ear of corn he'd been holding. "You will?" he exclaimed.

"Why not?" said Grandfather. He smiled at Benny. "I haven't been on a bicycle in a while, but I think I can remember how to ride it. It's something you never forget."

"That's great!" said Soo Lee.

"But what will you do for a bike, Grandfather?" asked Jessie.

"I can rent one at Greenfield Wheels," said Grandfather. "That shouldn't be any problem." He glanced around the table. "But you have to do your own fund-raising."

"We can do that," said Benny. He picked up his ear of corn and looked over at his grandfather. "You should eat everything on your plate," Benny told him. "And dessert. You have to get good and strong for the bike ride."

The next morning, the Aldens began thinking of ways to raise money for the bike ride. They started in the kitchen, right after breakfast.

"Soo Lee and I are going to have a lemonade stand. Mrs. McGregor said she could help us with the lemonade," said Violet.

"And we'll make a sign," said Jessie. "To put in front of the stand."

"While you are selling lemonade, we can ride our bikes to all the stores and ask for donations," suggested Benny. "That way, we can practice for the bike ride, too."

"Good idea," said Henry.

Using a wagon and with Henry, Jessie, and Benny helping, Violet and Soo Lee took the lemonade, a table, two chairs, cups, napkins, and a sign to a busy corner near their house. Watch trotted along behind, and when the table had been set up, he

sprawled out in the shade beneath it.

"Good dog," said Benny. "You stay here and help sell lemonade, Watch. We'll be back soon."

Watch thumped his tail in agreement.

Henry, Benny, and Jessie rode their bikes up and down the streets of Greenfield. Dr. Scott, the veterinarian who took care of Watch, made a donation. Sam, the ice-cream man, whose Clydesdale horse pulled the ice-cream wagon, made a donation, too.

But not everybody was as kind as Sam and Dr. Scott. The owner of the card shop, who was reading a newspaper at the counter when they came in to ask for a donation, listened with a stony face as they told him about Eagle Mountain. Then he raised the newspaper. "See this? This is May Whatney. She's a good customer and I'm not making a donation to you. That mountain doesn't need saving from her; it needs saving from people like you who are against progress."

"Thank you just the same," said Jessie politely.

"May your bikes all have flat tires," the man said. "Now go."

The Aldens left quickly.

"Wow," said Henry. "That wasn't any fun. I guess some people have very strong feelings about the Eagle Mountain issue."

"Yeah," said Benny. He made a face.

"Let's go in there," said Jessie, pointing at the antiques store. "I think Mr. Bellows will make a donation."

They were right. Will Bellows, like the veterinarian and Sam, had been part of one of the mysteries that the Aldens had solved and was happy to make a donation.

"So, are you going to solve any crimes on this bike ride?" Mr. Bellows asked.

"I don't think so," said Henry.

Jessie smiled. "We'll probably be too busy riding our bikes to think about any mysteries," she agreed.

"I bet we *do* find a mystery to solve," said Benny. "Just wait and see!"

CHAPTER 2

The Mean Limousine

A tanned boy with shaggy brown hair had just stopped at the lemonade stand as Henry, Benny, and Jessie arrived. He'd loosened the straps of his blue bicycle helmet and had it pushed back. He was wearing dark glasses and shiny black bicycling shorts.

"Hi," said Henry.

The boy scowled at them.

"Have some lemonade," suggested Jessie. "You look like you could use it."

"I changed my mind. I'm not thirsty," he said.

"It's for a good cause," Soo Lee said. "Did you see our sign?"

"I *know* about the ride," the young man said.

"We're all going to be in it," said Benny. "Even our grandfather."

But the young man wasn't paying attention to Benny. He was eyeing Henry. He pointed. "Is that your bike?" he asked.

"Yes," said Henry proudly. He'd bought the bicycle at a yard sale. It had been rusty and dented and missing its chain. Henry had repaired the bike. He'd given it a new chain, fixed the gears, and then he'd scrubbed away all the rust and painted the bike fire-engine red.

"What a hunk of junk!" the young man said.

Henry's face reddened.

"It's a beautiful bike!" declared Jessie, with her hands on her hips.

"Ha," said the boy. "You'll be lucky if you finish the first day of the race."

With that, he swung his leg back over his own sleek, shiny bicycle and pedaled away.

For a moment, everyone was too stunned to speak. Then Jessie said, "That's two rude people in one day."

"What else happened?" asked Soo Lee.

"When we were collecting money, we had one man who is a friend of May Whatney's practically throw us out of his store," Jessie explained.

"Grrr," said Watch.

"That's how I felt, too," said Benny, patting Watch.

"But he wasn't the only one you talked to, right?" Soo Lee said. "Did you raise any money?"

"We did," said Jessie. "Everybody else was pretty nice. What about you?"

"We almost sold out," Violet said proudly. "We have just enough lemonade left to give everybody a free glass." She poured out the lemonade and handed it around.

Benny finished his in one long gulp. "I'm hungry," he announced. "I need dessert."

That made Henry laugh. "Okay, Benny," he said. "You can have dessert. But first you have to eat lunch!"

After lunch, the Aldens counted their money. "We're getting closer to our goal, the entrance fees plus one dollar a mile," said Jessie, "but we still have a ways to go."

"I have an idea to raise more money," suggested Benny. "Let's have a car wash."

"It's worked in the past," agreed Henry. "It should work again."

The Aldens gathered sponges and buckets and soap. They took the lemonade sign and turned it over and wrote on the back, HELP SAVE EAGLE MOUNTAIN. HAVE YOUR CAR WASHED AND MAKE A DONATION.

They went out to the end of the driveway by the street. At first no cars stopped. Then a pickup truck pulled into the car wash. "I'll give you a big donation if you can get the back of my pickup truck clean," the woman inside said. "I've been hauling manure for my garden."

Violet wrinkled her nose. The truck smelled like manure.

But the smell didn't stop Henry. "You've got a deal," he said. The Aldens went to work.

Soon the whole truck was sparkling clean — and all of the Aldens were soaking wet. Even Watch, who wasn't very fond of baths, had somehow gotten wet.

"Good job," said the woman as Henry gave a side mirror a last polish with a dry cloth. She reached into her hip pocket, pulled out her wallet, and took out several bills. She handed the money to Violet and Violet gasped.

"Thank you!" Violet said. "That's the biggest donation we've had so far."

"A clean truck and a good cause," the woman said with a smile. "It's worth it." She waved as she drove away.

After that the Aldens washed a blue van, an old maroon Chevy, another pickup truck, and a station wagon.

Then a long black car pulled up to the curb. The window hummed down and a thin-faced man peered out from the driver's side of the car.

"How sweet," said the man. "But do you really think your little car wash is going to prevent people from taking Eagle Mountain to its full financial and developmental potential?"

"Well . . ." said Benny. He wasn't sure what the man had just said.

The man jerked his head in the direction of the bicycles propped against the front porch of the Aldens' house. "And I suppose those are the vehicles you plan to use in this bike race that's being talked about?"

"Those are our bikes," said Benny.

"We may not finish first, but every little bit helps," Jessie put in cheerfully. "Would you like us to wash your car?"

The man seemed to shudder as he answered, "I don't think so."

From the backseat, a woman leaned forward. The Aldens caught a glimpse of smartly cut brown hair streaked with blond and gray, and a pair of half glasses perched on the end of an upturned nose. "Ronald, that will do," the woman said.

"You don't want to make a donation, either?" Soo Lee asked.

The man called Ronald gave a snort. "Certainly not," he snapped. "Although it looks as if you could use one for those pathetic machines you call bicycles."

"That's enough. Drive on," the woman's voice commanded and she leaned back, disappearing from view.

"Yes, Ms. Whatney," Ronald said.

He rolled up the window and the car purred away.

"Ms. Whatney!" exclaimed Jessie, staring after the car. "So that's the developer who is trying to buy Eagle Mountain."

"And that man named Ronald must be her chauffeur," said Henry.

Violet said, "I guess she's very, *very* rich. She can probably pay lots of money for Eagle Mountain. How can we ever raise enough to stop her?"

She sounded unhappy. Henry patted her shoulder. "Don't worry, Violet. She's only one person and there are lots and lots of us who are raising money. And if we can show

how many people want the mountain saved, the governor might help, too. We'll be able to do it."

"I hope so," said Violet.

Just then, another car pulled up to the car wash, and the Aldens had to get back to work.

At the end of the day, they sat, tired and content, on the front steps of the house. "We can work on raising more money tomorrow," said Henry. "Maybe we can ride over to Silver City and see if we can get some donations there."

"That'll be fun. But I have to go home now," said Soo Lee. "I'll be back first thing tomorrow morning to help."

The Aldens worked hard for the next few weeks raising money and practicing for the ride. In the mornings they would ride their bikes, going farther and farther each day to get used to riding long distances.

Grandfather rented a bicycle from Greenfield Wheels and practiced with them often. Sometimes Soo Lee, Aunt Alice, and Uncle

Joe came along, too. Jessie put a special basket on the back of her bicycle so even Watch could come along. His legs were too short for him to run alongside during the long bike rides.

In the afternoons, the Aldens collected donations and held car washes and did chores for people in the neighborhood. They walked dogs and pulled weeds. They watered plants for people who went on vacation. They spent two days cleaning out a garage for a family that was moving.

Finally, two days before the race began, they sat on the front porch to count their money. "We did it!" said Jessie. "We have enough money for all of us, even Grandfather: entrance fees and one dollar per mile each."

Soo Lee sighed with relief. "Good. I was beginning to get worried."

"I knew we'd make it," Benny boasted.

"We even have a little extra," Jessie went on.

"The more money we have to help save Eagle Mountain, the better," said Violet.

Henry stood up. "Let's put the money away and go do some riding."

"Good idea," said Jessie.

"Not too far," Soo Lee warned. "Remember what Thelma told us. Right before the race we're just supposed to take short rides."

"We'll go to the park and back," said Henry.

"And tomorrow, we pack and get ready for the race," said Benny. "I can hardly wait. Then it will only be one more day. Isn't it great, Watch?"

Watch, who was standing beside Jessie's bicycle, wagged his tail. He was ready to go for a ride, too.

The Aldens pedaled away, with Watch hanging out of Jessie's basket, his ears flying.

"Eagle Mountain, here we come!" shouted Benny.

CHAPTER 3

Gone!

"Come on, Henry," Benny said the next morning. "We have to practice for the race one more time!"

But Henry didn't come out of the garage next to the house where the Aldens kept their bicycles.

"Henry?" Jessie called.

"I can't find it!" Henry said. His voice was muffled.

"Find what?" asked Violet. She leaned her bike against a tree and started toward the garage.

Just then, Henry burst out of the garage door. His eyes were wide. "I can't find it. I can't find my bicycle!" he cried.

"Isn't it in the garage?" asked Jessie. "I saw you put it there last night. You leaned it against the ladder."

Propping her own bike against Violet's, Jessie hurried toward the garage. Benny, Soo Lee, and Watch quickly followed. As soon as they walked into the old garage, Watch growled softly.

"What is it, boy?" asked Benny.

But Watch couldn't answer. He could only growl.

Jessie looked at the ladder in the corner where she'd last seen her older brother's bike. It wasn't there.

She glanced around the garage. She didn't see Henry's bicycle anywhere. She peered behind an old trunk. She raised the edge of a tarp, but found only spiders, dust, and a broken lawn mower beneath it.

The dust made her sneeze.

"It's not here," reported Violet, who'd been making a search of her own.

"Maybe you didn't leave it in the garage. Maybe we got yesterday mixed up with some other day. Maybe you forgot to put it away and left it out by the boxcar," Jessie said.

But as she spoke, Henry shook his head. "I'm sure I put it here last night," he said. "I never took it out to the boxcar."

"Then someone must have sneaked into the garage last night and taken it," said Violet. "But why?"

Henry shook his head. "I don't know. It wasn't worth much — except to me."

"We'll find your bike," said Jessie.

Suddenly she squatted down. "Look." She pointed to the track of a wheel through a patch of old motor oil on the floor of the garage.

"Any one of us could have made that track," Violet objected. "It's not the only one."

"But look how clear it is," Jessie said.

Henry bent forward. "You're right. That's the track of a new tire. You can see every ridge. All the other tracks are much

smoother, with many fewer tread marks."

"You're the only one of us who has a brand-new tire," said Soo Lee.

"And look at this!" Violet's voice rose in excitement as she pointed to the tracks leading from the garage.

The Aldens followed the tire track out of the garage. It curved suddenly and went off into the grass.

"The track leads out of the garage onto the grass at one side of the driveway, and I know Henry always goes straight up or down the middle of the driveway," Violet concluded.

"Why would someone ride your bike in the grass?" Benny wanted to know. "It's not a mountain bike. Is it?"

"No, it isn't," Henry said.

"Here's a streak of grease on the grass," Violet said from around the corner of the garage.

"That's funny," said Jessie. "It looks as if whoever took the bike wasn't taking it out to the road to ride away. He or she was going in the opposite direction."

"Then that's where we'll start looking," said Henry.

The five of them and Watch spread out and searched all around the big old white house. Henry checked the basement door just in case someone had moved the bike in there for a joke. But the door was locked from the inside, just as it always was.

Soo Lee suddenly cried, "Look!" She pointed to a slash of red on a large rock near the edge of the woods behind the Aldens' house.

"Is it blood?" gasped Benny.

"No," said Soo Lee. "I think it's paint."

Henry raced over, with Jessie and Violet close at his heels. He stooped and examined the red mark. "You're right, Soo Lee. It *is* paint."

"And it's exactly the same color as your bicycle," added Jessie.

"If the scrape is on this side of the rock, whoever took the bike was probably going in that direction," said Violet, pointing toward the woods.

"Maybe the thief made a getaway

through the woods?" asked Soo Lee.

"Then I guess we'd better look for more clues in the woods," Henry said.

"Let's spread out about five or ten feet apart," Jessie suggested. "That way we can cover more ground."

"Good idea," said Henry. "If anybody sees anything, shout."

"I will. Really loud," Benny said.

The Aldens began to search the woods. They crunched through the leaves and pushed aside branches. Benny and Watch found two rusty tin cans and an old pop bottle. Violet found a tattered plastic bag caught in some bushes. She and Benny put the cans and the bottle in the bag to throw away later.

Just when they were about to give up, Violet called out, "I see something red. Over there by that big tree."

Henry squinted in the direction she was pointing. "You're right, Violet," he called back. "Let's go."

He and Violet pushed through the bushes. A moment later, Jessie, Soo Lee,

Benny, and Watch heard Violet wail, "Oh, no!"

"Let's go!" shouted Jessie, and led the rest of the search party to Henry and Violet.

They all stopped and stared in stunned silence at what lay in the small clearing beneath the big old oak tree. It was Henry's bike — or what was left of it.

"Who would *do* such a thing?" Soo Lee asked.

"I don't know," said Henry in a choked voice.

The tire on the rear wheel was flat, and several of its spokes were broken. The paint was scratched and scraped. Dirt clogged the gear wheels and bike chain. The chain itself was snapped. The bottom of the front fork, which held the front wheel on the bike, was bent.

"Oh, Henry," said Violet. "I'm so sorry about your bike."

"Me too," said Henry.

"Maybe whoever took it ran away in such a hurry that it got all beaten up in the woods," said Soo Lee.

Jessie said, "Well, whoever took this bike didn't seem to care what happened to it."

"Maybe we can get it fixed," said Benny. "Let's take it to Greenfield Wheels."

"I guess we can try," said Henry.

With Jessie's help, Henry carried the bike out of the woods. They told Grandfather what had happened and he called the police to report the theft. Then they all walked slowly into town. As they walked, they tried to figure out what had happened.

"Maybe it was Ms. Whatney and her driver. Ronald, that was his name," said Violet. "Maybe they wanted to keep us from riding in the race."

"It could be," said Henry. "After all, it's Ms. Whatney who wants to buy Eagle Mountain."

"And she knows where we live," Benny added.

"And Ronald the chauffeur even asked about our bikes," said Soo Lee.

"Maybe it was one of the people who were so mean to us when we were raising money," said Violet.

"Like that guy who made fun of Henry's bike in front of our lemonade stand," said Soo Lee.

"Or the man at the card shop who told us he hoped we'd all have flat tires," Benny said.

Henry sighed. He said, "It could be any of those people, I *guess*. But it doesn't really make sense and we don't have any proof."

"When people do mean things it usually *doesn't* make sense," Violet added softly.

Henry looked sadly at his battered bicycle and added, "And now I don't have a bicycle for the race."

CHAPTER 4

Ready, Set, GO!

"We'll get it fixed," declared Jessie. "Louis at the bike shop said that Thelma can fix anything."

"She *might* be able to fix it," said Henry, looking a little more hopeful.

The Aldens walked with Henry and his broken bicycle into Greenfield to the bike shop. But this time, when Louis popped out from the repair room in the back, his eyes widened in surprise. "Your bike!" he said to Henry. "It looks as if a car backed over it."

"Maybe one did," Henry answered

glumly. "We're not sure what happened. Can you fix it?"

"Hey, we're the best bike shop around. We can fix anything," Louis said. He turned and called, "Thelma!"

"Coming, coming, coming," said Thelma. She walked out and stopped short. She looked at the wrecked bike, then at Henry. "I hope you were wearing your helmet when you were in the bike accident," she said in a stern voice.

"We always wear our helmets," Henry said. "But I'm afraid my bike had the accident without me." He told the bike shop owners the story. "So can you fix it for me before the race?" Henry concluded.

Thelma said, "Fix it, yes. Before the race, no."

"No?" repeated Henry. His shoulders slumped.

Thelma and Louis exchanged glances. Then Louis spoke up. "I tell you what," he said. "We'll lend you a bike for the race."

Henry's face brightened. "You will?"

"We will," said Louis. "We rent bikes, you know, and we have several good, solid bikes that should do fine during the race. We'll find one just right for you."

As he spoke, Louis rolled a bike out from behind the counter.

"That's got *two* seats!" objected Benny.

"It's a bicycle built for two people," Louis explained. "It's called a tandem. And this is a special tandem, because the backseat and pedals of the bicycle can be adjusted to a smaller size."

"Smaller like me?" Benny asked.

"Exactly," said Louis.

"So Henry and I could ride together?" asked Benny.

"That's the idea," Louis agreed.

"It's a *good* idea," said Benny. He leaned toward Louis as if he were telling him a secret. "You know, my legs get a *little* tired on the long bike rides."

"I thought they might," Louis said with a smile. "This should solve the problem."

"Is it expensive to rent?" asked Jessie.

Thelma said, "No. I think you'll find the

price is just right. We'll put our store's name on the bicycle. And we'll give you all T-shirts with our store's name on them, too. You wear the T-shirts on one of the days of the race, and you can use the bike for free!"

"Really?" said Violet.

"We get free advertising. You have a bike to ride. What could be better?" Louis said.

"Thank you," said Henry.

"Hooray!" said Benny. "Come on, Henry. Let's go get ready for the race!"

Benny and Henry waited while Louis adjusted the back pedals, then they rode the bike home to practice on it. Jessie, Violet, and Soo Lee walked home, carrying the new T-shirts. The front of the shirts had bicycle wheels in all different sizes on them. The backs of the shirts said, THELMA AND LOUIS AT GREENFIELD WHEELS SAY "KEEP ON PEDALING!"

The children went on a short bike ride and then Soo Lee rode her bike home to pack for the race. They planned to get up very early the next morning to make sure they were at the starting line on time. So they finished packing right after dinner and got ready to go to bed early.

But first they went outside to check on their bicycles. Henry rattled the lock on the garage door, just to make sure it was fastened.

"I'm not taking any chances," he said. "Whoever did it might come back and take someone else's bike."

"Or our new tandy," said Benny.

"Tandem," corrected Jessie.

"I'm going to call the bike Tandy," said Benny. "That way I can remember."

"Tandy it is," said Henry.

Violet sighed. She looked up at the pale stars that were just beginning to come out. "I wonder who took your bike, Henry. And why."

Henry sighed. "This is one mystery we may never solve."

"Well, we shouldn't worry about that now," said Jessie. "Now we just need to get a good night's sleep, so we can get to the bike race on time."

*   *   *

"We got here early," said Violet the next morning. "And so did everybody else!"

The Alden children, their cousin Soo Lee, and their grandfather stared around at the crowd of bicyclists and spectators. The bikes and the riders came in all shapes and sizes. Bike helmets of every color bobbed up and down in the crowd.

Reaching into her pocket, Jessie patted the envelope. "I think I'd better go turn our money in," she said.

"We'll come, too," said Violet, glancing at Soo Lee. Soo Lee nodded.

Grandfather took Benny's hand. "We'll go and get us all signed in," he said.

"I'll stay under this oak tree with our bicycles," Henry said. "We can meet back here."

Henry sat down by the bicycles to wait. He yawned. He leaned back. They had gotten up *awfully* early that morning. His eyelids began to close.

"Hey! Wake up, sleepyhead!" Jessie said.

Henry sat up with a jerk. "I wasn't asleep," he protested.

"Yes, you were. Anyone could have just ridden off on one of our bicycles," teased Soo Lee.

But Henry didn't laugh. He jumped up and inspected the bicycles anxiously. They were all there and they were all fine. He sighed with relief.

"Attention, riders," came a voice over a loudspeaker. "The ride will begin in fifteen minutes."

"Uh-oh!" said Jessie, sounding worried. "Where are Grandfather and Benny?"

But just then Grandfather and Benny appeared. Benny was skipping with excitement. "We all get numbers," he said. "We put the big numbers on our bicycles, and we stick the little numbers on our helmets, one for each of you and one for me," he explained.

Benny handed the numbers around.

Grandfather gave out maps and explained the rules. "I've handed in our sleeping bags and gear," he said. "You just show your number and they'll give them back to you at the end of the ride each day. And remember, every rider has to be in camp by half an hour before sunset. If you don't make it by then, the sweep wagon will pick you up."

"The sweep wagon?" asked Benny.

"It's a van to pick up riders who can't finish the ride each day," explained Grandfather, "either because they are too tired to go on or because their bikes broke down. If you have to ride in the sweep wagon during the ride, you aren't eligible for the raffle for the new bike at the end."

Just then, the man with the microphone began to speak. "Attention. You all have maps. The route will also be marked with signs that look like this." He held up a sign that looked like the jagged peak of a mountain, in bright lime green. To one side of the sign was a red arrow. "Just follow the arrows and you won't get lost. We'll have water stops at the places marked on the map. And of course, you can stop and rest anytime you want. Remember, this isn't a race to beat everyone else, but a race to save our mountain!"

Cheers broke out.

The man smiled and nodded. Then he directed the riders to begin to line up behind the starting line. "I'll blow the whistle in about five minutes. When I do, the ride will begin. Keep in mind the rules of safety, and remember: You MUST wear your helmets at all times."

Eagerly, the riders began to wheel their bikes toward the starting line.

Suddenly a bicyclist near them glanced over and said, "What are *you* doing here?"

Henry looked up. The voice sounded familiar. It was the bicyclist who'd stopped by the lemonade stand and made fun of Henry's bike. Henry stared at the boy hard. Was this the person who had stolen his bike and ruined it?

He said, "We're riding in the bike race, just like you."

The boy's eyes dropped to Henry's bike. "Well, well, well. A *tandem*. How . . . interesting. At least it's not an old bomb like that red bike of yours."

Benny scowled fiercely at the boy. But

before anyone could speak, a girl just ahead of the boy turned. "Don't be such a poor sport, Al," she said in a cool voice.

Al's cheeks reddened.

The girl went on, "You're no one to talk. Your bike isn't all that great."

"Who asked you, Nan?" Al muttered.

He tried to push his bike away from them, but the crowd was too thick.

The girl smiled at Henry and Benny. "I'm Nan Bellini. Al and I are in the same bike club. Sometimes I let him beat me in bike races."

"I'd beat you all the time if I had a bike like yours," said Al. "Or like the bike they're raffling for this ride."

"It's not the bike, it's the rider," Nan retorted.

"Your bike is beautiful," said Jessie.

"You think so?" Nan looked down at her bike with a little frown. She shrugged. "It's okay, I guess," she said. "It's not titanium or anything."

"Almost as pretty as the one Henry had," insisted Benny. "I'm Benny Alden, and that's Henry, and my sister Jessie. Oh, and there's my sister Violet and my cousin Soo Lee and my grandfather. Our dog couldn't come. He's waiting for us at home in Greenfield. But he wanted to come."

Nan laughed. "You can take him to the park, though, after you save it."

"We will," said Benny. He liked the idea.

Glancing at Henry, Nan said, "What happened to your bike?"

They told Nan what had happened. When they finished, she shook her head. "That is awful," she said. "Who would do that to a bike? And to another bike rider! Only the worst kind of person. A true bike creep!"

"Yes! A bike creep!" repeated Benny. He liked the sound of it. "A big, *mean*, bad-sport bike creep!"

Al muttered something they couldn't hear and forced his bike through the crowd away from them.

Laughing a little, Nan said, "Speaking of people who might be bike creeps, isn't that May Whatney over there?"

They all turned to stare across the crowd. Sure enough, standing by her car was Ms. Whatney and her chauffeur, Ronald.

"That's Ms. Whatney, all right," said Henry. "And her chauffeur, Ronald."

"I wonder what she's doing here," Jessie said, half to herself.

Ms. Whatney was staring at the riders, her expression more curious than angry. Beside her, Ronald was talking and gesturing. Just then, a man in a thin windbreaker split at one elbow, wearing a backward baseball cap and dark glasses, stopped at Ms. Whatney's other side. The three of them talked for a few minutes. Then the man drifted away.

"Maybe she's trying to sabotage the race, the same way someone sabotaged your bicycle, Henry," said Violet.

"Could be," Henry said. "After all, she only wins if we *all* lose."

"I gotta go," said Nan.

The man with the microphone hopped up on the chair. "Riders!" he called. "Fasten your helmets."

The crowd of bicycle riders grew quiet.

"Are you ready?" the man called out.

"Yes!" roared the riders all together. Cheers broke out. Jessie put two fingers to her lips and let out a piercing whistle.

The man raised his air horn. "Go!" he shouted and blew a blast on the horn.

The riders surged forward. Henry let out a whoop. Benny hunched over and began to pedal furiously.

The great bike race had begun.

CHAPTER 5

On the Road

Wheels whirred and gears clicked as the swarm of bicyclists pedaled along the swooping road that led out of the park. The early morning sun danced over the riders. Violet and Soo Lee spun along the road side by side.

As they reached the entrance to the park, the riders began to spread out more. Violet saw a ribbon of riders filling one side of the road all the way up the next hill. A quick glance back told her she had just as many riders behind her.

"Coming through! On your left!" Jessie called out cheerfully. She passed Violet and Soo Lee, waved, and disappeared around the curve ahead with a group of cyclists.

"We're right behind you," Henry said. "You're looking good, Violet, Soo Lee."

"Thank you," said Violet.

"Grandfather's near the back," reported Benny. "He said he was going to take it easy for a while."

"That's what Soo Lee and I are going to do, too," said Violet.

"Not Jessie, though," said Soo Lee, laughing. "I think she's too excited to go slow yet."

They pedaled onward. They met a few cars, but it was too early for many to be on the road. A dog sat at the end of his driveway and barked at them as they went by.

A girl on a bicycle delivering morning newspapers waved and shouted, "Helloooo! Good luck!"

They passed farms and empty fields and ponds and heard roosters crowing from barns and hen yards. As they passed one house, a sprinkler began to spray water over the front lawn.

"I'm thirsty," Soo Lee said.

"Me too," said Benny.

Soo Lee reached down and took her water bottle off the holder on the frame of her bicycle. She kept pedaling as she squirted water into her mouth.

The sun rose higher. The roosters stopped crowing. Near the front of the riders, Jessie almost finished her water bottle. She wiped her sweaty face and kept going.

Then she saw someone holding a sign. It was a thin girl with a shirt that said RIDE VOLUNTEER. As each bicyclist approached her, the girl waved the sign. It said, FIRST WATER STOP AHEAD! YOU'RE DOING GREAT!

"Oh, good," gasped Jessie. She could get water and refill her bottle.

The water stop had been set up in the parking lot of an office building that was closed for the day. Jessie followed the arrows tacked to the trees and turned into the lot. A few bikers were leaving as she got there, but many more were behind her.

Members of the volunteer support crew had set out paper cups on rows of tables while other crew members were getting more jugs from the truck.

Jessie got off her bike and leaned it against a tree. She unbuckled her helmet and pushed it back. She wiped her forehead and squirted the very last of the water from her bottle over her hot face and sweat-soaked hair. Then she got her water bottle and headed for the refreshment table that had just been set up near her. She grabbed a cup of water that a volunteer had just poured out of a big jug and gulped down a giant swallow. Other riders were eagerly gulping down cups of water all around her.

"Oh, no!" shouted a volunteer. "What kind of a bad joke is this?"

He gestured at the jugs of water and fruit juice that volunteers were unloading from the truck. "All the jugs are either empty or leaking."

Sabotage, thought Jessie, but she didn't say it aloud. She saw Nan arrive, jump off her bike, and go over to one of the jugs

of water. She opened the spigot and held her water bottle underneath to refill it, but nothing came out.

"Hey!" she said. "This jug is empty."

At that moment Benny, Henry, Violet, and Soo Lee came into the water stop. "I'm *so* thirsty. I could drink a million gallons of water!" Benny declared.

"You might not get anything to drink, Benny," said Jessie.

"What do you mean?" Benny asked.

A gray-haired woman in a cap that said CREW CAPTAIN on it put her hands on her hips and said, "Almost all of our jugs are empty! Someone opened the spigots while they were in the truck."

"They must have done it after we got here," another crew member said. "The jugs were filled when we left."

"Well, whenever it was done, we don't have enough water for the riders!" the crew captain said. "It's all on the floor of the truck."

Sure enough, a thin sheet of water was pouring out of the back of the truck.

"Maybe there's a water fountain in the building," Henry suggested.

But the building was locked.

Other riders rode into the water stop.

"We have to find water somewhere. We can't let the riders go thirsty, especially on such a hot day," the crew captain said.

"I have extra water," came Grandfather's voice. He was standing by his bike, holding a water bottle that he had taken from his backpack. "I can share."

"Me too," said someone else.

"I have some, too," said a third. "And some juice."

Soon all the riders who had water were sharing it with the riders who didn't. Along with the coolers that still had water in them, there was just enough water for everyone to have a drink.

"That's wonderful," the crew captain said as she watched all the riders sharing water.

"We'll find more water along the way, anyway," said Al, who was standing near the end of the table. He clipped his empty bottle into his bottle holder and swung his bike out of the water-stop parking lot.

Other riders began to follow. The parking lot emptied out.

"I'm still a little thirsty," Benny said softly. But he got on the bike behind his older brother. They went up one hill and down another and Benny thought of how Watch panted on hot days when he was thirsty. He tried panting, but it didn't help.

They rounded a curve. By the side of the road ahead was a clump of riders.

"Oh, no," Violet said anxiously. "I hope no one had an accident."

But it wasn't an accident. As they slowed to a stop, they saw water squirt into the air in the midst of the stopped riders.

Someone laughed. Someone else said, "Feels good."

"Missy! Don't squirt people! Help me fill their water bottles," said a girl with dark braided hair. She looked down at a smaller girl, who also had dark hair, in pigtails.

The smaller girl grinned, showing a missing front tooth. "Okay," she said. She held a garden hose out and directed water into each rider's bottle.

The Aldens saw that the two girls had brought the hose from the front of their house to fill water bottles for the riders. As each bottle was filled, the older girl said, "Good luck," and the younger girl echoed her words. Their mother watched proudly from the porch of the house.

"Thank you," said Benny to the younger girl as she filled his bottle.

She looked at him in surprise. "How old are you?" she asked.

"Six," said Benny.

"Me too," the younger girl said. "Good luck."

"Thanks," said Benny, waving as he and Henry pedaled away.

They kept riding. Then Jessie, who'd sprinted ahead, slowed down. She stopped her bike.

Her family stopped with her. She said, "Up ahead, beyond that hedge — isn't that Ms. Whatney's car?"

"I think it is," said Henry. "I think we should ride by extra slowly and take a look."

Sure enough, the car belonged to Ms. Whatney. They could see her in the back, talking on a phone.

She didn't see them. But Ronald did. He was leaning against the front fender, watching the riders pass.

He surprised all of the Aldens as they went by, however. He didn't frown or scowl at them. Instead he smiled.

Then he raised a cup to his lips and took a long drink. "Hot day," he said. "Having something cool to drink sure is nice, isn't it?"

CHAPTER 6

A Bad Sign

"That was so mean of him," said Jessie angrily as soon as they were out of his hearing.

"I know. He shouldn't make fun of us for being thirsty," said Soo Lee.

"Well, he doesn't like us. Or the bike race," Henry said.

"And maybe he's the one who emptied all the water out of the jugs," said Violet. "Maybe he and Ms. Whatney did it."

"He *was* wearing a navy blue T-shirt, almost the exact same color as the crew members'," Violet said.

"He could have slipped up onto the truck and into the back of it and opened all the spigots," Jessie said. "I wonder if anybody noticed anything suspicious."

"We can ask when we reach the riders' camp tonight," said Benny. "And look for clues."

"I think that is an *excellent* idea," agreed Henry. "But first we have to get there."

At the next stop, in a small park by a river, the Aldens found lunch waiting for them and all the riders.

"This is good," said Benny, eating the graham crackers he'd found in the lunch bag he'd taken off a lunch table. "And look! An orange. And a sandwich. *And* the sign says I can go back for seconds."

"I don't think we have to worry about you going hungry on this ride," said Henry, smiling at his younger brother.

"No," agreed Benny happily. "And now there's plenty of water, too."

He and Henry ate slowly. Grandfather, who had been riding in the back, came to join them. But Soo Lee, Violet, and Jessie finished quickly.

Jessie jumped up. "Let's get going!" she said. "I'm not tired anymore."

"Having lunch helped," agreed Soo Lee.

Violet stood up and stretched. "You want me to wait with you?" she asked her brothers and grandfather.

"Go on ahead," Henry said. "We'll catch up with you later."

"Okay," said Violet. She threw away her trash from lunch, fastened her helmet, and followed Soo Lee and Jessie out of the picnic grounds.

The riders were more spread out now, pedaling in clumps of two or three. They stopped more frequently to rest.

They passed a mileage marker and Violet checked her map. "We don't have much farther to go," she said.

"Good," said Soo Lee. "We'll get to camp in plenty of time, and we won't have to ride in the sweep wagon."

"Yeah," said Jessie. "No sweep wagon for me!"

They rode on. And on. The sun began to go down. Violet's legs ached and Jessie had finished all her water. Soo Lee gave Jessie some of her water, but Soo Lee's bottle was getting low on water, too.

Violet slowed to a stop. "We haven't passed any other riders in a long time," she said.

"We must be way ahead of them," said Jessie.

But Violet shook her head. She said, "We haven't passed the last water stop, either. We should have reached that by now. And we haven't seen anyone along the side of the road with signs to cheer us on, like we did before."

"There's another arrow," said Soo Lee. "It's pointing straight ahead." Then she said slowly, "Wait a minute." Soo Lee walked her bike up to the sign. She leaned over to look at it. She could see it was torn at the corners — it must have been stapled down. But there weren't any staples on the old wooden post. Instead, the paper had been stuck hastily on the end of a rusty nail.

"This sign looks like it came from somewhere else," she said. "As if it had been just torn off and placed here."

"You're right!" said Jessie.

Violet had pulled out her map. She studied it. She looked up. "We're supposed to be on County Road Eighteen," she said.

Jessie said, "Uh-oh." All three of them turned to stare at the street sign they had just passed. It said ROUTE 76.

Henry, Benny, and Grandfather waited by the entrance to the camp. Henry kept looking at his watch. Benny waved and cheered as a rider pedaled slowly in.

"It'll be dark soon," said Henry. "Where can they be?"

"They'll be here," Grandfather said.

Henry glanced at his grandfather and Benny. He was sure Grandfather was right. He had nothing to worry about. But he couldn't help it. He knew how fast Jessie had been riding. And all three of them had

left right after lunch. He hadn't seen them since then.

"If they had a flat tire or bike trouble, wouldn't we have passed them on the road?" he said.

"Maybe they stopped for water at someone's house," Benny said. "And we passed them then and didn't see them."

"Maybe," said Henry.

Grandfather said, "Even if they are having problems, the sweep wagon will pick them up."

"Not the sweep wagon!" Benny said. "Then they can't be in the raffle."

The sun was down. It would be dark soon. A few riders were still trickling in as the other riders who had gathered cheered them on.

A crew member said to another crew member, "I bet the next thing we see is a sweep wagon full of riders."

"You're right. I see it, just coming over that hill way up the road," said the other crew member.

"Jessie!" cried Benny, jumping up and down.

Sure enough, Jessie came pedaling into the camp. Right behind her were Soo Lee and Violet.

Jessie pulled to a stop and spun to look back down the road. "We beat it!" she gasped. "We beat the sweep wagon."

She, Violet, and Soo Lee were all breathing hard.

"What took you so long?" Henry asked.

"We were getting just a little bit worried," put in Grandfather.

"Got lost," panted Soo Lee. "Tell you about it at dinner."

"Dinner," said Benny. "Where's dinner?"

"This way, Benny," said Grandfather.

"I'll show you where to check your bikes at the bike corral," said Henry. "And walk you to your tents. They're right across the row from Grandfather's and mine."

"I'm staying with you, Jessie," said Benny.

Jessie managed a smile.

The sweep wagon rolled into camp and the crew began to close the camp gates.

Jessie turned. Her eyes widened. "It's a whole tent city," she said. "It's huge."

"I guess you'd better show us around, Henry," said Violet, "or we might get lost again!"

Grandfather smiled and took Benny's hand. "We'll meet you at dinner," he said.

"Someone changed the signs," Jessie concluded. She, Soo Lee, Henry, and Violet stood in a long, long line that snaked from the dining tent all the way across the park where the tent city had been set up.

The line hadn't moved in a long time. Some of the riders had sprawled in the grass, waiting for dinner. The last light of day was fading in the west.

"We weren't the only ones who got lost," Violet said. "But we met the others on our way back and told them, and they turned around. So they didn't have to ride as far as we did."

"Sabotage," said Henry. "Someone wanted you to get lost. Or to not finish."

"Maybe they wanted to wreck the whole ride," said Benny.

"Maybe — " Violet broke off. "Look,"

she said. "Remember that man we saw this morning, talking to Ms. Whatney and Ronald? He just walked out from behind the dining wagon. And he's headed this way."

The man was still wearing his scruffy coat and backward hat. He walked slowly, his eyes traveling over the tent city: the riders, the tents set up for dining and repairing bicycles and selling Eagle Mountain T-shirts. The man saw the Aldens watching him and raised his eyebrows.

The outdoor lights came on, and now they could see him clearly. He was older than he had first appeared to be.

"Are you a rider?" Benny blurted out.

"No," said the man. "But I can see that you all are. How's it going?"

"We've had some bad luck today, but it's fine," said Jessie stoutly.

The man's eyebrows rose higher. "Bad luck? You've had good weather. Looks like a great volunteer crew."

"Not enough water at the first stop," said Henry. "Someone sabotaged it." He watched the man closely as he spoke. The man didn't appear surprised.

"Really," he said.

"And someone put up signs that made us get lost," Soo Lee said. "We almost didn't make it back to camp before the sweep wagon."

"Oh?" the man said.

"And someone stole my brother's bike the night before the race and wrecked it," Benny put in.

"Hmmm," said the man, looking at Henry. "But you're here."

"The bike shop gave us a tandy bike," Benny explained.

Now the man changed expression. He looked puzzled.

"A tandem bike," Henry explained. "Lent to us by our bike shop, Greenfield Wheels."

"Ah," said the man. "Well, you've had some tough luck. But it could be worse." He drew back one corner of his mouth in what might have been a smile and walked away.

"He's weird," said Soo Lee.

"Definitely," agreed Jessie.

"Do you think he sabotaged the water and moved the signs?" Henry mused. "Nothing we told him seemed to surprise him."

"You're right," Jessie said, staring after him. The man went around the corner of a tent and, following two signs that said BIKE CORRAL and INFORMATION TENT, he disappeared.

Jessie shivered. "Did you hear what else he said?" she asked. "He said, 'It could be worse.' That sounded like a threat."

"It did," Soo Lee said softly. And although it was a warm night, she shivered a little, too.

CHAPTER 7

"I'm Hungry!"

A grumble went down the line. A crew member ran out of the dining tent, followed by another. They raced past.

"I don't believe this," one of them said as she ran by.

"What's going on?" asked Benny.

A moment later, another member of the dining hall crew walked down the line. "Dinner will be delayed," he announced as he walked. "Come back when we ring the bell. It will be at least an hour."

"What's wrong? What happened?" Jessie inquired.

The crew member shook his head. "We got everything set up. We were ready to unload the food and start dishing it out. And then we discovered that someone had tampered with the lock on the food wagon."

"It's broken?" asked Violet.

"No. Looks like someone put glue in it. It's going to take a locksmith to get it open," he answered. He shook his head again. "I just hope the food doesn't spoil."

"Me too!" said Benny.

Henry said, "Did you see anybody suspicious around the food wagon?"

"Ha," the crew volunteer said. "Like anyone would have time to notice. We've all been too busy to notice *anything*."

"I'm *hungry*," said Benny.

"I have some snack bars in my tent, Benny," said Soo Lee. "You can have one."

"Maybe we could all have one?" Jessie asked hopefully.

"There might be enough to go around," Soo Lee said. "Let's see."

They went back across the park to the tents. Soo Lee had enough snack bars for everybody. She even had one left over. They took the snack bars to a picnic table over-looking a small pond.

"If I had my fishing pole," said Benny, "we could catch fish and cook them for din-ner. I wonder who put glue in the lock? I guess whoever it was, wasn't very hungry."

"Whoever it was is trying to sabotage the ride," said Henry. "Too many things have gone wrong."

"Your bike. The water mess at the first rest stop. The fake directions. And the glue in the lock," said Violet, counting each one on her fingers. She held up four fingers.

"Wow. And we haven't even started the second day of the ride yet," said Soo Lee.

"Who could it be? Do you think whoever wrecked your bike is the same person who did everything today?" asked Jessie.

Henry said, "Well . . . it could be. After all, Al came by the lemonade stand and knew which bike was mine. And he was at the water stop this morning when we got there."

"That's right," said Jessie. "He could have gotten there early and slipped in and opened the spigots."

"Or it could have been Ms. Whatney and Ronald. He knew about the water and he was glad it happened. And he was right there, remember?" Soo Lee pointed out.

"And they could have driven ahead in their car and changed all the signs around," Henry said.

"Or the mysterious stranger could have done it," Benny said. "With the backward hat. He knows Ronald and Ms. Whatney. And we saw him walking away from the mess tent tonight."

Henry rubbed his forehead. "They all seem suspicious, don't they? But Ms. Whatney wants to buy Eagle Mountain and make money by cutting down the trees and putting up a resort, so she has a reason."

"Or it could be someone else," said Violet.

"But how do we figure out who did it?" asked Soo Lee.

"We'll have to watch everyone very carefully from now on," said Henry. "Tomorrow, Benny and I will keep an eye out for Ms. Whatney and Ronald."

"And the mysterious stranger," said Violet. "Soo Lee and I will help."

Soo Lee nodded distractedly. She was looking in the direction of the dining tent.

"And I'll ride extra fast and try to stay near Al to keep an eye on him," Jessie promised.

Soo Lee stood up.

"Soo Lee? What is it? What's wrong?" asked Violet.

Soo Lee grinned. The sound of a bell floated through the early evening dusk.

"Dinnertime!" she announced.

But their troubles weren't over. Soon after dinner, the lights went out in the camp. Soo Lee and Violet, who had been brushing their teeth, had to hurry, shining their

flashlights up and down the rows of tents to find their own.

Other flashlights crisscrossed the rows of tents as other riders looked for their sleeping spots. Each row had a letter and each tent had a number.

"N," whispered Violet. "Here's our row."

"We're near the end," Soo Lee reminded her. As they walked past the tents, they could hear people talking in soft, sleepy tones. Everyone was tired.

They stopped in front of their tent. Violet crawled in, then Soo Lee followed. Soo Lee leaned out. "Good night," she called softly to Henry and Grandfather, and to Jessie and Benny, who were in the tents across from Soo Lee and Violet.

Behind her, Violet said, "Sleep tight."

"I will," said Benny, his voice muffled.

"Night," called Jessie.

Grandfather and Henry didn't say anything. The only sound that came from their tent was a quiet snore.

Violet pulled up her sleeping bag. Soo Lee snuggled down into hers.

"Good night, Violet," whispered Soo Lee.

"Good night, Soo Lee," Violet whispered back.

She turned off the flashlight and yawned.

And then she screamed as something dark and smothering swooped down on her.

"Help! Help!" cried Violet, thrashing her arms above her head.

"Oh, oh, oh," shouted Soo Lee, punching and kicking.

"Ow!" said Violet as Soo Lee kicked her in the leg.

"Ouch!" said Soo Lee as one of Violet's thrashing arms caught her in the shoulder.

"It's okay, it's okay," Henry's voice came to them through the darkness. "Your tent collapsed."

Struggling out of the tent with Soo Lee, Violet became aware that they weren't the only ones who'd been kicking and shouting for help.

Violet blinked. "Wha-at?" she managed to say.

"It's not just your tent," Jessie announced. "It's the whole row. Look at that."

Now volunteers came running with flash-lights.

"Just a tent problem, folks," a woman called as she hurried along. "The night crew will fix it in no time."

"Look at this," Jessie said. She had gone to the end of the row. The Aldens followed her voice until they found her. She had her flashlight pointed down at something on the ground. "It was deliberate. Someone made those tents all come down on purpose. All the rear tent pegs at this end of the row have been linked together with a single piece of thin rope looped over each peg. Whoever did that only had to yank the rope and all the rear tent pegs came up. Boom. The tents collapse," Jessie said.

Henry squatted to examine the rope. "Just plain cord," he said. "But whoever did this is pretty smart. It's simple and quick. All he — or she — had to do was walk by and pull. No one would even notice."

As Henry had predicted, no one had. Dozens and dozens of bikers had been up and down the rows of tents since they were put up. "Anyone could have tied the pegs together," said Henry.

"Not anyone," said Violet. "It had to be someone staying in the tent city. Remember? They closed the gates."

"That rules out Ms. Whatney and Ronald, then," said Jessie.

Soo Lee said, "That's right. Only riders and crew members and volunteers are allowed to stay in the tent city."

"Maybe Ronald sneaked in," said Benny. He yawned. "Or maybe the backward hat man."

"Or maybe it *was* Al," said Henry softly.

They walked back to their tents and helped put them back up. Soon the camp had settled down again. People began to fall asleep.

But Henry and Jessie lay awake in their tents, trying to figure out who wanted to sabotage the bike race, and why.

"Oh, good. No glue in the locks this morning," said Benny.

A yawning crew member shuffled by and

heard Benny's words. She smiled wryly. "That's because we left someone on guard," she said. She shook her head. "We have strict security to guard the bicycles in the corral. No one allowed in without their bike number and race ID pass. But who thought we'd have to guard the food?"

She yawned hugely and said, "I need a shower," and broke into a trot toward the shower wagons.

The Aldens quickly ate their breakfast of cold cereal, juice, and muffins, and headed for the bike corral. On the way, they ran into Nan.

"Hey," she said. "How's it going?"

"Okay," said Henry. He didn't feel like talking about everything that had gone wrong.

Nan fell into step beside him.

Henry looked down. "What happened to your leg? Did you fall off your bike?"

A large new bruise was on Nan's shin. It was purple and shiny.

"I bumped into something last night," she said.

"Why didn't you use your flashlight?" Violet asked.

Nan made a face. "Well, it was late. I didn't want to wake people up. I thought I could find the bathrooms in the dark."

"You're lucky you didn't fall into someone's tent," said Soo Lee with a little laugh. "Our tents fell last night."

"Was that the noise I heard? I'm all the way at the end of the tent city, so I couldn't tell what it was," Nan said. She showed her rider identification and race number to the corral volunteer.

They were among the first riders to get there. The volunteer guard waved them through.

Nan walked straight down the rows toward her bike, but it took the Aldens a little while to find theirs. When they did, they discovered that something was wrong.

"Hey," Benny said. "This isn't my helmet. My helmet doesn't have pink stripes on it!"

"My helmet's not orange and silver," said Henry.

"This helmet's the wrong color and the

wrong size," said Soo Lee, turning to show a helmet that was sliding down over her nose.

"All our helmets have been mixed up with other people's," said Violet.

"Not just ours," said Jessie. "Look!"

As bikers poured into the bike corral, voices were raised all around them in indignation. Several rows of helmets, which had been tied to the bikes during the night, had been switched around.

For the next hour, noise and disorder ruled. Cyclists ran up and down the row, peering at helmets and waving the ones they had above their heads.

Henry finally found his helmet and the owner of the one that had been attached to his bike. He helped Benny locate his helmet while Violet, Soo Lee, and Jessie looked for theirs.

"What about Grandfather?" asked Violet suddenly. She had just found her own helmet, much to her relief. "I'll see if he needs help finding his helmet."

But the helmets on Grandfather's row, much farther away, hadn't been switched around.

Violet also couldn't help but notice that the helmets on the row where Al had his bike hadn't been switched, either. All the riders in his row of parked bicycles were calmly picking up their helmets and putting them on.

Then Violet noticed something else: The man with the backward hat was standing just inside the entrance of the bike corral, staring at the rows of bicyclists trying to find their helmets. He had his hands in his pockets and no expression at all on his face.

As if he felt Violet staring, he turned. He smiled at her, that funny jerk of the corner of his mouth.

Violet gave him a halfhearted wave, ducked her head, and hurried back to join the others.

As they walked their bikes out of the corral after finally finding her helmet, she told her family what she had seen.

"It does seem a little suspicious that Al's row didn't have any mixed-up helmets," said Jessie.

"And why did the mystery man suddenly turn up just as it all happened?" Benny wondered out loud.

No one knew the answer to that. And the mysterious man was gone when they reached the entrance of the corral. The Aldens looked around, shrugged, and then rode out of the camp to begin the second day of the great bike race.

CHAPTER 8

An Unexpected Helper

"Uh-oh," said Henry, just after they left the second water stop.

"Are we lost?" asked Benny. "I know how to get back to the water stop."

"We're not lost," said Henry, pulling the tandem to a stop. "We have a flat tire."

He got off. Benny got off. They squatted down to look at the tire. It was very flat. "Looks like we picked up a piece of glass," said Henry. He got out the tire-changing kit and went to work.

"Can I help you?" Nan asked, slowing her own bike down.

"Hmmm," said Henry, prying the tire off the wheel. He pulled the tube out from the inside. If he replaced the tube inside the tire, the tire wouldn't be flat. The tube was what held the air in the tire, and the tire protected the thin tube.

"Why don't you try to patch that tube and I'll put the new tube in for you to save time," Nan said.

"Thanks," said Henry.

"No problem," Nan answered. "I've changed about a million tires."

As Benny watched, Henry patched the old tube and folded it into the tire patch kit he carried strapped under the back of the bicycle seat. Nan finished putting the tube and tire back on and jumped up. "Keep your tire pressure low," she said. "That'll help avoid flats."

"Will do," said Henry. "Thanks again."

"Glad I could help," Nan said. She swung her leg over her bike and pedaled away.

As Henry got back on his bike, Violet

and Soo Lee rode up. "Is everything okay?" Violet asked.

"We're fine. Just a flat tire," said Henry.

They rode on, enjoying the sunshine and the farms and woods they passed. The bike riders wandered on back roads through hills and fields. But today, since they weren't as anxious and excited as they had been on the first day of the race, they had time to notice more.

Many people had turned out to cheer them on. Children stood at the foot of their driveways waving. The bicyclists saw signs tied to trees and mailboxes. They passed a three-person family band in front of one house: a boy playing the trumpet, a girl playing the drums, and a very little boy banging on a saucepan with a spoon.

The Aldens waved and smiled and shouted hello as they rode by. None of them wanted to stop any more than they had to. They wanted to be sure they made it into camp in time that night.

Shortly after lunch, Henry slowed to a stop.

"What's wrong?" asked Jessie.

"Flat tire," Henry said. "Again." He made a disgusted face.

He and Benny stopped the tandem. "I'm getting good at this."

He took out the tube. It looked as if it had gotten pinched between the rim of the wheel and the tire. Henry shook his head. "It's a nasty hole," he said. "I think I'll wait to fix it until tonight to save time and put my patched spare on now."

"Yes. Let's hurry. I don't want to ride the sweep wagon," Benny agreed. He looked nervously around. But they were a long way ahead of the sweep wagon.

Henry smiled at his younger brother. "Don't worry," he said.

He went to work on the flat and soon he and Benny were back on the road again.

But not for long. They pedaled up a hill and slowed as they reached an intersection. A sign in the intersection said, ROAD CLOSED. DETOUR.

Henry was about to turn down the road when he felt a familiar *bump, bump, bump.*

"Oh, no!" he cried. "We have another flat."

"*You* have a bad-luck tire," said Benny.

"I think you're right," Henry said.

"I'm doing everything Nan told me," Henry said. "I don't have any spare tubes. I just hope I can . . ." His voice trailed off as he saw the tube. It had caught between the wheel and the tire, just like the last time. The hole in the tube was a big one.

"Oh, no," said Henry under his breath.

A bike pulled to a stop beside him.

"Can I help?" came a voice Henry knew. He looked up in surprise.

It was Al.

"A flat tire," he said. "It's pretty bad."

Al looked at the tube. "Yeah, those snake bites can be nasty."

"Snake bites?" asked Benny, alarmed.

"That's what cyclists call it when the tube gets caught between the tire and the wheel rim. It usually happens when you don't put enough air in the tube."

"Oh," said Henry.

"Fortunately I have a spare tube," Al said. "You can have it."

"Thank you," said Benny. He sounded amazed.

Al's cheeks reddened slightly. "I guess you wouldn't know that, with an old bike like you had. I mean, those tires had a different kind of tube in them and — "

Henry got very still. "How would you know that?" he asked.

Al's cheeks grew redder. "Just a guess," he said.

Henry looked steadily at Al. Al wouldn't look at Henry.

Then Henry said quietly, "You're the one who wrecked my bike, aren't you?"

Staring hard at the tube he was fitting into the tire, Al said, "Yes."

Benny jumped up. "That was mean!" he shouted. "And . . . and really, really bad."

"I know," Al said. Now his ears were red. "I'm sorry. I know it was a horrible thing to do. I didn't mean to wreck the bike. I ran into a tree. I was just going to leave it in the woods until the race was over. It was stupid and wrong."

"And you let the water out of the jugs, and you changed all the signs and made the tents fall, and — "

"No!" Al raised his head. "*No!*" he shouted. "I didn't do any of those things. I've been trying to be better. I don't want to be a bad sport. After I heard what Nan said at the start of the race, I realized what an awful thing I'd done. I'm sorry."

That stopped Benny. He folded his arms. "Well," he said. "You should be."

"Anyway, I'm going to pay for fixing it. Or to replace it, if it can't be fixed," Al went on. He gave Henry a hopeful look. "Will you let me?"

"Yes," said Henry. "Thanks."

"Thank you," said Al, jumping up. "And your tire is fixed. Just remember to keep a lot of air in that tube, and you shouldn't have any more snake bites."

He fastened his helmet and was about to ride away when a police car pulled up. An officer got out, shaking her head. "Kids," she said. She looked over at the three boys. "Did you move this detour sign?" she asked.

"No!" said Henry, Al, and Benny in unison.

"Well, I'm moving it back down the road where it belongs. And if you know who did this, tell them it's not funny," she snapped. Lifting the sign, she tossed it in the trunk of her car and drove away.

"That's the wrong way, then," said Al.

"I guess so," said Henry.

"I wonder how many riders ahead of us went in that direction," Al said.

"Someone changed the signs, just like yesterday," said Benny.

Al said, "I'm going to ride to the next water stop and let them know. They can send some of the crew to catch up with any riders who might have gone the wrong way."

"Good idea," said Henry.

Without another word, Al jumped on his bike and pedaled off — in the right direction.

Henry and Benny followed. As they reached the rest stop, they saw Ms. Whatney's car pulling out. It turned and went back in the direction from which they had just come.

"I wonder where they're going," Benny said.

Henry wondered, too. But he didn't talk much for the rest of the afternoon. He was too busy thinking about who could have changed the sign — and who was really behind all the bad luck that kept threatening to ruin the ride.

Not until they were almost at the camp did Henry speak. "Benny," he said. "Al wrecked my bike, but he didn't do any of those other things."

"I know," said Benny. "Wait until we tell everyone."

"I have something else to tell everyone," said Henry.

"What?" asked Benny.

"I think I know who's behind everything that has gone wrong with the great bike race," said Henry.

CHAPTER 9

Henry's Plan

The Aldens stood at the day's finish line, applauding as the last riders came in ahead of the sweep wagon.

"I'm glad we didn't follow that detour sign," said Jessie. "Getting lost two days in a row would have been too much."

"Not so many people got lost this time. And what a surprise. It was Ms. Whatney who caught up with the ones who had followed the sign and got them to turn around before going too far out of their way," said Henry.

"And Al didn't switch the signs today," Benny said. "He was with us. He *did* say he wrecked Henry's bike, though."

"I've told you I think I know who is behind all of the trouble now," said Henry. "And I've got a plan."

"What? Tell us!" Jessie pleaded.

"Follow me, and I'll tell you while we walk," Henry said.

At the bike corral, the crew member who was standing guard at the entrance didn't ask any questions. "The guard tonight?" he said. "Anna Wong. You could check for her in the volunteer tent section. Or leave a message on the volunteer message board there."

"Thanks," said Henry. They found Anna Wong emerging from her tent, yawning and stretching.

She stopped yawning as Henry introduced himself, and the Aldens told their story. When they had finished, she said, "I can do that. I'd like to catch whoever's behind all this, believe me. I love Eagle Mountain."

"We'll meet you at dinner, then," said Henry.

"And don't forget — we've never met before," Jessie reminded her.

Anna pushed her short dark hair back from her face and laughed. "I can't remember," she said. "And I won't have to pretend too much to be sleepy. I still am."

Shortly after that, Henry led the Aldens through the dining tent. They passed several empty tables, but none of them seemed to suit him.

Then Violet whispered, "Over there."

"Right," said Henry. He walked in the direction that Violet had indicated and sat down at an empty table.

Anna Wong appeared almost immediately, carrying her dinner.

She slowed as she got nearer. Henry tipped his head toward the back of the person sitting at the next table across from the Aldens.

Anna nodded back. She walked over, slid her dinner down at the place in front of Henry and just behind the person he had pointed out, and said, "Do you mind if I sit here?" She yawned loudly as she sat down.

"Please join us," Violet said.

"I'm Benny," Benny said, and introduced the rest of his family.

"I'm Anna Wong," Anna said. She yawned even more loudly. "I'm on the crew."

"Hard day?" asked Soo Lee. "You seem tired."

"I *am* tired," Anna said. "I'm on bike corral guard duty tonight. I just hope I can . . ." She let another yawn interrupt her and then finished, ". . . stay awake."

"Were you on duty last night, too?" asked Violet.

"No. Someone else was. I just hope nothing happens tonight. It would be terrible. I would feel awful," Anna said.

"You'll do fine," Jessie reassured her.

"I hope so," Anna said. "I go on duty right after lights out. I just hope I don't go on duty and then go to sleep." She finished her sentence with the loudest yawn of all.

They ate in silence for a while. When they all finished, Benny spoke first.

"I'm getting sleepy," Benny said. He yawned.

"We'd better head back to our tents," Jessie said. She stood up. The rest of the Aldens did the same.

"Good luck tonight," said Violet politely.

"Thanks," said Anna. And winked.

The figure of Anna in the darkness had been drooping in the chair by the corral entrance. Now her head tipped back and she started to snore. Loudly.

The snoring went on, then stopped. Anna shifted, mumbled, and pulled her hat down over her eyes to block out the light by the gate where she was keeping watch. The field of bicycles inside the enclosure was dimly lit by the lights that had been placed around the fence.

Then she began to snore again.

Time passed. Anna appeared to be in a deep sleep.

From their hiding place behind a nearby rock, the Aldens watched. Behind them, bicycle riders and volunteers slept in the rows of tents. It was quiet and dark except for the beam of an occasional light as a rider made a cautious late-night trip to the bathroom or to get some water.

Violet clutched Henry's arm and whispered, "I saw something move. Over there!"

Benny almost jumped up to peer over the rock, but Jessie caught him in time. "Not yet, Benny," she hissed.

They kept waiting. Sure enough, Violet had been right. They saw a tall, slender figure emerge from the shadows. It edged toward Anna's sleeping form.

Looking left and right, the shadowy figure hesitated for a moment outside the bike corral. Then it eased the gate open just a fraction and slipped inside.

"Come on," said Henry.

Crouching low, the five Aldens hurried to where Anna still appeared to be sleeping.

"Shout when you're ready," Anna said softly. "I'll throw the switch and turn all the

corral lights on." She spoke without moving from her position of seemingly deep sleep.

"Right," Jessie said.

One by one, the Aldens slipped inside the gate.

Jessie said, "Benny, why don't we take this side of the corral."

"We'll take the other," said Henry. He, Soo Lee, and Violet disappeared into the shadows at the edge of a bike row.

Keeping down and moving cautiously, Benny and Jessie did the same. At the end of each row, they stopped and peered cautiously down it.

Suddenly Benny said, "I see someone."

"Let's go," said Jessie. "On this side of the row, so we can't be seen coming."

She and Benny raced down the row, trying to move as quietly as possible. They slowed as they heard a sound — a click, and then a pop. After each click and pop, the figure moved to the next bicycle.

"The spokes. They're being cut on each bicycle," Jessie breathed.

Benny didn't wait. He jumped to his feet, turned his flashlight on, and shouted at the top of his lungs, "Stop that!"

The lights of the bicycle corral turned on full force. Anna Wong popped out of her chair and began running down the middle aisle of the rows of bicycles. Henry, Violet, and Soo Lee began running from the other side of the corral.

And Nan gave a little shriek, dropped her wire cutters, and tried to run.

CHAPTER 10

Journey's End

"Oh, no you don't," said Henry. He caught Nan's shirt.

She yanked and twisted, but it was too late. Benny grabbed one leg and the others surrounded her.

Gasping and red-faced, she stopped. "I didn't do anything," she said. "I was just checking on my bike."

"With these?" Jessie asked, holding up the wire cutters.

Anna had been inspecting the damage. "About ten bicycles have at least one cut

spoke," she reported. "Our repair people can fix that."

"How many spokes were you going to cut?" Violet asked.

Nan's friendly smile was gone. She pressed her lips together and said, "It didn't damage the bicycles permanently. Spokes can be fixed."

"You're the one who leaked the water at the first water stop," Jessie said.

"No, I didn't leak the water. I would never do anything to harm a rider's health!"

"But you *did* change the signs so the riders would get lost," Soo Lee said. "You were ahead of us. You could have done it easily."

"And you rigged the row of tents so it would fall," Henry said. He pointed. "You got that bruise sneaking around in the dark last night. And you changed the detour sign today. And I bet you put glue in the lock on the food wagon, too."

"And what about switching the helmets?" said Benny.

"You can't prove any of it," Nan muttered.

"I can prove that you sabotaged me,"

Henry said. "You told me the exact opposite of what I should do to fix my flat tire. That's the reason I kept getting flats — because I wasn't putting enough air in my tires."

"So?" Nan's eyes shifted.

"So you'd do anything to eliminate as many riders as possible from this ride," Violet said. "To win that raffle."

"You won't win it now," Anna said. She motioned and the Aldens saw flashlights in the dark and realized that other crew members were headed for the corral. "I doubt you'll be allowed to finish the ride."

Nan drew herself up to her full height. "Fine. I did all that. It was you who gave me the idea, when I heard you talking to Al about your bike getting sabotaged. Why not sabotage a few more riders? The fewer who finished, the better chance I had at that bike. And I need a new bike. A really good new bike. With a really good bike I could win races and lots of prize money. . . ." She let her voice trail off as several crew members approached. One of them had a shirt on that said, SECURITY CREW CHIEF.

The security chief folded her arms as the Aldens and Anna told her what had happened. When they'd finished, she turned to Nan.

"I think we'd better take a look at your bike kit, Nan," she said.

Reluctantly, Nan took them to her bike and the security crew chief looked in the small pouch of emergency tools most cyclists keep just behind their seat.

"Just as I expected," she said as she drew from the small leather pouch a tube of glue.

"That's not bike patch glue. That's what she used to glue the lock on the food wagon," said Benny.

"And how do you explain these?" continued the security chief, looking at Nan sternly. In her hand she held four packets of raffle tickets. It looked as though they had all been filled out with Nan's name. "I'd be willing to bet we'll discover some missing raffle tickets."

"Wow," said Jessie. "There are twenty-five tickets in each pack. That's a hundred tickets. If those were somehow all put into the raffle at the end of the race . . ."

"*And* if dozens of riders had gotten lost — and disqualified — by following the wrong signs . . ." said Henry.

"*And* if more riders got discouraged and quit the race because of late food, collapsing tents, and no water . . ." continued Violet.

"Nan would have a pretty good chance of winning the new bike at the raffle. Right?" finished Benny.

"Right," said Jessie quietly.

The chief of security turned to Nan. "What do you have to say for yourself?" she asked.

With a toss of her head, Nan said, "Nothing. I'm going to be a famous bike rider someday, and to get famous you have to be tough."

"But not mean and stupid," the security chief said. "And what you did was mean-spirited and stupid. Let's go. We're going to pack up your stuff and escort you out of here in the sweep van. You're out of the ride."

Anna spoke up. "The rest of us will fix these spokes."

"Good," said the chief. She turned to the Aldens and nodded. "And good work," she told them.

"Thank you," said Benny modestly. "We solve mysteries all the time. If you ever need us to solve another one, we live in Greenfield. We — "

"Benny, let's go get some sleep," Violet said, patting her little brother's shoulder.

"Okay," said Benny. He looked at the others solemnly and added, "It's important for a bike rider to get lots of sleep. Especially if he's going to solve mysteries, too."

"Eagle Mountain is saved!" Jessie announced as she led the way into Greenfield Wheels two days later.

"There was a huge crowd at the end of the race," Violet said. "And the governor made a speech!"

"I know. I heard," said Thelma. "Congratulations."

"And your bike is ready, Henry. And paid

for. A young man came in *very* early this morning and insisted on taking care of the bill," Louis said.

Henry was glad Al had done what he'd promised.

"We didn't win the fancy bicycle," Soo Lee said. "Someone else did."

Benny said, "But we got to use this tandy." He patted the bicycle that he and Henry had brought to the store to return.

"Good," said Louis.

"And we solved a mystery, too," Benny said.

Thelma gave Benny a sly grin. "I don't guess you're going to tell me about it, are you?"

"Oh, yes," said Benny. But it wasn't just Benny who told the story of the great bicycle race while Thelma and Louis listened and asked questions and exclaimed in amazement.

When the Aldens had finished, Thelma said, "There's one thing I don't understand. Who leaked the water the first day?"

Jessie said, "Ronald, Ms. Whatney's

chauffeur. When she heard what had happened, she remembered him stopping at the water wagon. He thought he was doing what she wanted him to do, but it turned out he was wrong."

"She fired him!" Benny cried.

"I'm glad of that," Louis said.

"And the mystery man?" asked Thelma.

"With the backward hat?" Soo Lee said. "That's what Benny called him, the backward-hat man. He worked for the governor. He was observing the ride for her. His report is one of the things that helped persuade the governor to save the park."

"How did you find that out?" Louis wanted to know.

"We saw him talking to her," Violet explained. "And we just went up and asked him."

Thelma laughed. "I'd say solving a mystery is just a matter of asking the right questions," she said.

Henry said, "And setting the right trap."

Benny had wandered away to look at the bike shop bulletin board. He called out,

"What does this say?" and pointed at a brightly colored sign.

Violet went to the bulletin board. "It's about another bike ride," she said. "In California. Five nights, six days."

"Wow," Benny said. He clapped his hands. His eyes sparkled. "When is it? Should we start practicing now?"

"Oh, Benny," Jessie said.

Benny grinned. "What?" he said. He put his hands on his hips. "I *like* to bike race. And solve mysteries, and I'm ready for the next one!"

"Even if someone puts glue in the lock of the food wagon again and dinner is *hours* late?" asked Violet.

Benny frowned and stroked his chin thoughtfully for a moment, then broke into a grin. "Maybe we can bring our own food," he suggested brightly.

The bike shop rang with the laughter of Violet, Jessie, Henry, and Louis and Thelma.

"What's so funny?" he asked. "You know you can't solve a mystery on an empty stomach!"

GERTRUDE CHANDLER WARNER discovered when she was teaching that many readers who like an exciting story could find no books that were both easy and fun to read. She decided to try to meet this need, and her first book, *The Boxcar Children*, quickly proved she had succeeded.

Miss Warner drew on her own experiences to write the mystery. As a child she spent hours watching trains go by on the tracks opposite her family home. She often dreamed about what it would be like to set up housekeeping in a caboose or freight car — the situation the Alden children find themselves in.

When Miss Warner received requests for more adventures involving Henry, Jessie, Violet, and Benny Alden, she began additional stories. In each, she chose a special setting and introduced unusual or eccentric characters who liked the unpredictable.

While the mystery element is central to each of Miss Warner's books, she never thought of them as strictly juvenile mysteries. She liked to stress the Aldens' independence and resourcefulness and their solid New England devotion to using up and making do. The Aldens go about most of their adventures with as little adult supervision as possible — something else that delights young readers.

Miss Warner lived in Putnam, Connecticut, until her death in 1979. During her lifetime, she received hundreds of letters from girls and boys telling her how much they liked her books.